Dear Parent:

Congratulations! Your child is taking the first steps on an exciting journey. The destination? Independent reading!

STEP INTO READING® will help your child get there. The program offers five steps to reading success. Each step includes fun stories and colorful art. There are also Step into Reading Sticker Books, Step into Reading Math Readers, Step into Reading Write-In Readers, Step into Reading Phonics Readers, and Step into Reading Phonics First Steps! Boxed Sets—a complete literacy program with something for every child.

Learning to Read, Step by Step!

Ready to Read   Preschool–Kindergarten
• big type and easy words • rhyme and rhythm • picture clues
For children who know the alphabet and are eager to begin reading.

Reading with Help   Preschool–Grade 1
• basic vocabulary • short sentences • simple stories
For children who recognize familiar words and sound out new words with help.

Reading on Your Own   Grades 1–3
• engaging characters • easy-to-follow plots • popular topics
For children who are ready to read on their own.

Reading Paragraphs   Grades 2–3
• challenging vocabulary • short paragraphs • exciting stories
For newly independent readers who read simple sentences with confidence.

Ready for Chapters   Grades 2–4
• chapters • longer paragraphs • full-color art
For children who want to take the plunge into chapter books but still like colorful pictures.

STEP INTO READING® is designed to give every child a successful reading experience. The grade levels are only guides. Children can progress through the steps at their own speed, developing confidence in their reading, no matter what their grade.

Remember, a lifetime love of reading starts with a single step!

*For my nieces,
Kirsten and Erica
—J.M.*

*To my parents
—R.R.*

Text copyright © 1985 by Joyce Milton. Illustrations copyright © 1985 by Richard Roe.
All rights reserved under International and Pan-American Copyright Conventions. Published in
the United States by Random House Children's Books, a division of Random House, Inc.,
New York, and simultaneously in Canada by Random House of Canada Limited, Toronto.
www.stepintoreading.com
Educators and librarians, for a variety of teaching tools, visit us at
www.randomhouse.com/teachers
Library of Congress Cataloging-in-Publication Data
Milton, Joyce.
Dinosaur days / by Joyce Milton ; illustrated by Richard Roe.   p.   cm. — (Step into reading.
A step 3 book)
Originally published: New York : Random House, c1985.
SUMMARY: Brief and simple descriptions of the various kinds of dinosaurs that roamed the
earth millions of years ago.
ISBN 0-394-87023-9 (pbk.) — ISBN 0-394-97023-3 (lib. bdg.)
1. Dinosaurs—Juvenile literature. [1. Dinosaurs.]
I. Roe, Richard, 1959– ill.   II. Title.   III. Series: Step into reading. Step 3 book.   QE861.5.M55
2003   567.9—dc21   2002013222
Printed in the United States of America   90 89 88 87 86 85 84 83 82 81
STEP INTO READING, RANDOM HOUSE, and the Random House colophon are registered trademarks
of Random House, Inc.

STEP INTO READING®

STEP 3

DINOSAUR DAYS

By Joyce Milton

Illustrated by Richard Roe

Random House 🏠 New York

There are no dinosaurs today.

Not even one.

But sometimes

people find dinosaur bones.

The bones are like
parts of a puzzle.
When they are put together,
you can see
what a dinosaur looked like.

The word <u>dinosaur</u> looks hard.

But it is really easy to say.

Say: DIE-nuh-sor.

<u>Dinosaur</u> means "terrible lizard."

Millions of years ago

the world belonged

to the dinosaurs.

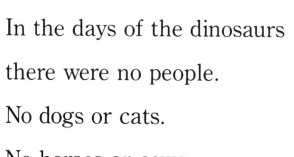

In the days of the dinosaurs

there were no people.

No dogs or cats.

No horses or cows.

What animals were there?

Turtles.

Crocodiles.

Fish.

Dragonflies.

The world was very warm

and very wet.

11

One of the very first dinosaurs

to live on earth

was named Saltopus.

SAWL-tuh-puss

Saltopus lived near a river.
The river was full
of giant crocodiles.

When these giants got hungry,

they came after Saltopus.

SNAP! went the giants' jaws.

SNAP! SNAP!

Then Saltopus stood up

on its strong back legs

and ran away as fast as it could.

Saltopus was fast.

It could run and leap.

That is how it got its name.

Saltopus means "leaping foot."

Saltopus was a small dinosaur.

About the size of a chicken.

Dinosaurs came in many sizes.

Some were small like Saltopus.

Some were big.

And some

were very, very big.

One of the biggest
was Brontosaurus,
also known as
Apatosaurus.
BRON-tuh-SOR-us
uh-PAH-tuh-SOR-us

This dinosaur was
as tall as a house,
longer than two buses,
and as heavy
as five elephants!

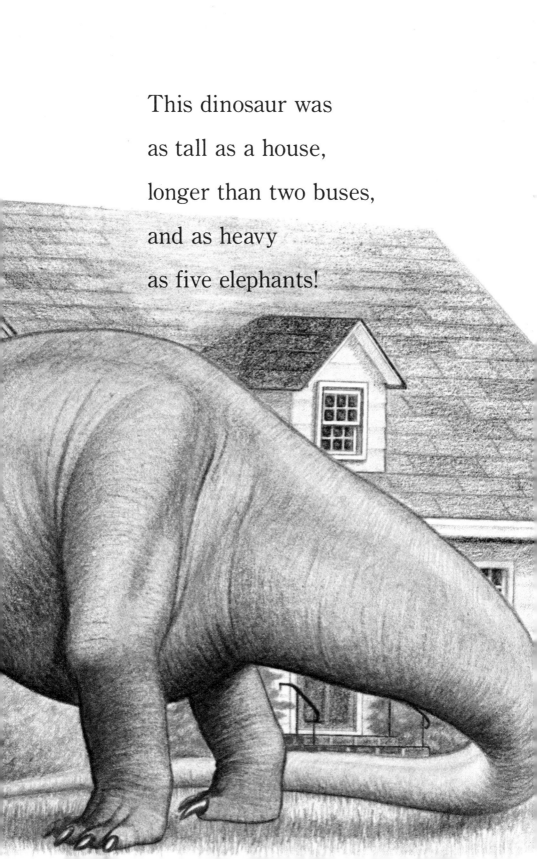

The name <u>Brontosaurus</u>
means "thunder lizard."
When Brontosaurus went walking,
its great big feet
made a noise like thunder.
Brontosaurus ate plants.
Lots of them!

Other dinosaurs
hunted for meat to eat.
One meat eater
was named Allosaurus.
AL-uh-SOR-us

When a hunter dinosaur
came around,
what did Brontosaurus do?
One thing it could do was hide.
Where? Under water!

This dinosaur was fat and slow.

It could not run and hide.

But it did not need to!

Its back was covered
with thick plates.
Its tail was covered
with sharp spikes.
Its name was Stegosaurus.
STEG-uh-SOR-us
That means "covered lizard."
It was one
of the early dinosaurs.

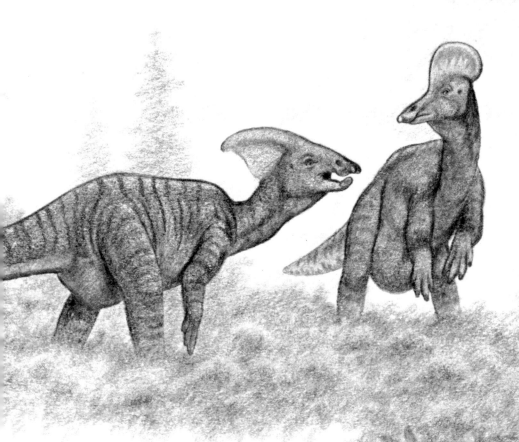

Not all kinds of dinosaurs

lived at the same time.

Early kinds

like Brontosaurus

died out.

And new kinds

took their place.

Some of the newer dinosaurs
looked a little like ducks.
They are called
duck-billed dinosaurs.

This duck-billed dinosaur
is called Anatosaurus.
an-AT-uh-SOR-us
That means "duck lizard."

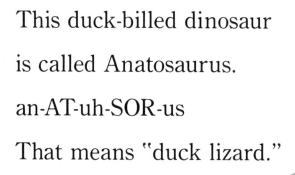

Anatosaurus had lots of teeth.
Two thousand of them!
It used its teeth
to mash up plants.

What dinosaur

had the biggest teeth of all?

Tyrannosaurus Rex.

tie-RAN-uh-SOR-us REKS

Its teeth were as long as pencils
and very, very sharp.
The word <u>rex</u> means "king."
This dinosaur was the king
of the hunters.
What did it hunt?
Other dinosaurs!

Some dinosaurs

had ways to keep safe

from Tyrannosaurus Rex.

This dinosaur

had hard plates on its back.

The plates were like armor.

When danger was near,

it just sat tight.

The name of this dinosaur

is Ankylosaurus.

an-KIE-luh-SOR-us

Ankylosaurus also had

a strong tail.

It could swing its tail

like a club.

This dinosaur
used its sharp horns
for fighting.
When it came running,
everyone got out of the way!

Its name is Triceratops.

try-SER-uh-tops

That means "three horns on the face."

There are many things

we do not know

about the dinosaurs.

We think most of them

were brown or green.

But we don't know for sure.

Maybe some were brightly colored.

We do know
how dinosaurs were born.
They hatched from eggs,
just like baby birds!

Some dinosaur eggs
were big...
bigger even than a football.
But some were only the size
of a potato.

This dinosaur

is named Protoceratops.

PRO-tuh-SER-uh-tops

The mother made her nest in the sand.

She laid many eggs at one time.

Did she sit on the eggs?

Probably not. She was too heavy.

The eggs might break!

When the babies were born,

they were very small.

Much, much smaller

than their parents.

You could hold

a baby Protoceratops

in your two hands.

In the days of the dinosaurs

strange animals

lived in the sea.

They were real-life sea monsters.

Some of these monsters

looked like dinosaurs.

But they were not dinosaurs.

They were called Plesiosaurs.

PLEE-zee-uh-SORS

They had long necks.

They reached into the water

to catch fish.

Other strange animals
flew in the air.
One of these animals
was Pteranodon.
ter-AN-uh-don
Its body was no bigger
than a turkey's.
But its wings were as wide
as the wings of a small plane.

Pteranodon flew far out to sea.

It rested on the tops of waves.

When it took off,

it soared on the wind

like a glider.

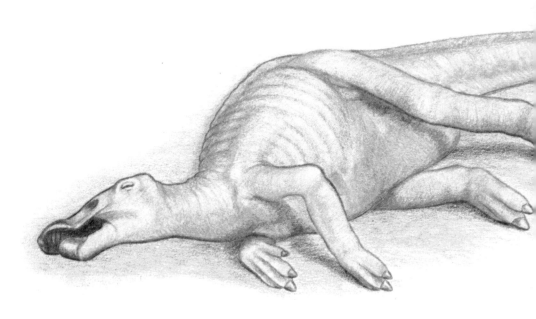

The days of the dinosaurs

lasted a very long time.

Millions and millions of years.

Then a time came

when there were no dinosaurs.

What killed them all?

Maybe the world got too hot.

Maybe the dinosaurs could not find

the right food to eat.

Maybe other animals

ate the dinosaurs' eggs.

Some people even think

the trouble was caused

by a comet

that came too near the earth.

No one knows for sure
what happened.
But in time new animals
took the place
of the dinosaurs.